PELOPS

The Making of the King

AF619954

PELOPS

THE MAKING OF THE KING

Clive Hagon

Copyright © 2020 by Clive Hagon

All rights reserved. This book or any portion thereof may not be reproduced or used in any manner whatsoever without the express written permission of the publisher except for the use of brief quotations in a book review or scholarly journal.

First Printing: 2020

ISBN 9781916382206

Clive Hagon
Suite 320, 2 Lansdowne Crescent
Bournemouth BH1 1SA

www.bronznehousepublications.com

cover design: J Ferrando

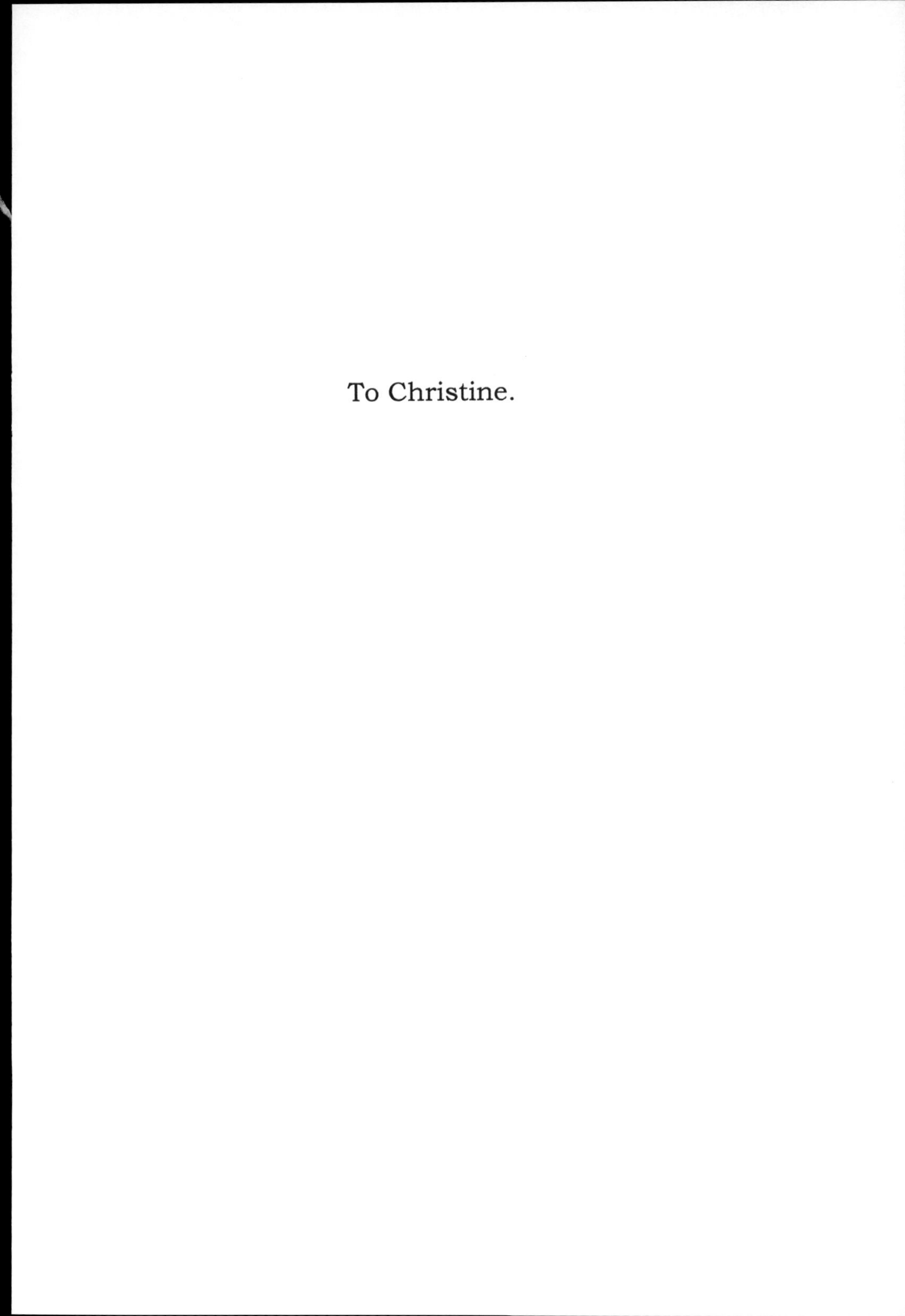

To Christine.

Once upon a time, long, long ago, the gods of Olympus made Tantalus king of Sipylus. The kingdom, rich in the minerals copper and tin, necessary for the manufacture of bronze, made Tantalus wealthy beyond any other mortal being. Zeus, who was the father of Tantalus, invited his son to dine with the gods in his home at Olympus. During the meal, Tantalus descended into intoxication, and, in his state of drunkenness, stole nectar and ambrosia from his host.

Tantalus, at first pleased with his accomplishment, began to resent the gods of Olympus for their immortality, their beauty, and their wisdom. His resentment simmered into envy, then boiled over into seething animosity. Tantalus was seized by a desire to bring them down to the level of mortal beings, and he formed a plan to prove them ignorant. As gods they had the power of foresight and could divine the reality of all things. He invited the deities to a feast in his hall and he served them a casserole made from the flesh of his own son, Pelops. Most of the guests, aware of the origin of the meat, did not touch the food, but Demeter, distraught at the loss of her daughter, Persephone, absentmindedly ate part of the boy's shoulder and swallowed his left shoulder blade.

The gods were outraged by this atrocity, and bound Tantalus in chains. As punishment he was cast down to Hades, where he stood in a pool of water that was surrounded by trees bursting with fruit. When hunger demanded gratification, he would reach for the fruit, but the trees would pull back their branches and deny him satisfaction.

When driven mad with thirst, he would stoop to drink the fresh water in which he was stood, but each time he sought to drink, the water receded, and he remained parched. For eternity, Tantalus was tantalized, tormented by his own lusts.

The gods of Olympus so loved Pelops that they reconstructed his body from the parts salvaged from the casserole, and the parts that Demeter vomited up. The butchered flesh was gathered, but the left shoulder blade had been digested by Demeter. Hephaestus forged a new shoulder blade from ivory, and Clotho placed the gathered flesh and the ivory shoulder blade in a cauldron. She boiled the cauldron, stirred the pot, and span forth a reconstructed Pelops.

So beautiful was the newly formed youth, that Poseidon fell in love with him and conveyed him to his home at Olympus. Poseidon made Pelops his apprentice charioteer and taught the boy the skills of the great masters. Zeus, however, harboured resentment, a bitterness against the heir of Tantalus, and, still enraged by the foul actions of his mortal son, flung Pelops from the heights of his new home.

Pelops span and tumbled as he fell through the air. From the heights of Olympus, through the clear clean air, he crashed into the stone-strewn ground, his body shattered on the rocks, his skin grazed on the gravel. He lay still for a long time.

*

Circling high in the frigid air, a lone vulture, his belly aching with hunger, espied the fallen body. For three days, since his last feed, he had cruised the high thermals, searching, with increasing desperation, for meat. From a mile above, through the clear air, the sight of the fallen carcass filled his black heart with gluttonous intent. Determined not to lose this fresh feast to a rival, he dropped with the speed of gravity, and with the intent of the ravenous.

The body, sprawled on the barren earth, remained still. The vulture drew near. He could smell the blood that oozed from the wounded flesh. He could taste the bile rising in his throat. He drew close, poised.

The hand that encircled the vultures throat moved with such speed that he had no time even to squawk. With a twist his neck snapped, and the creature folded into the dirt. Pelops opened his eyes, rolled onto his side, and bit deep into the dead bird. He ate his fill.

Fortified by the meal, Pelops looked around. Far in the distance, the snow-capped Mount Olympus touched the blue sky. What had once been his home was home no more. He turned away his gaze. "If I am to live as a mortal man", he reasoned, "then I should seek them out, and live as one with them". As he spoke, even to himself, he found his voice grating. What had once been music to his ears now sounded harsh. He shrugged away the thought. As he stood, his legs strained against the pain of the multitude of grazes. His left arm was stiff, unbending, pointing forward, his fingers fused, so that they, opposed to his thumb, looked like a claw. With his first step he stumbled and strained for balance. He tried to stand upright, but his back would not respond. He remained hunched in hideous deformity.

Pelops sat on a rock and reflected upon his situation. His life at Olympus had been a life of beauty. He had feasted on ambrosia and quenched his thirst with nectar. The voices of his companions rang with sweet tones, and he had replied with the voice of music. His body, light as a cloud and radiant with the glow of health, had resonated with the landscape as if he were an integral part of some vibrant orchard. Now, through no fault of his, he was cast down into ugliness. Hunger had driven him to eat the raw flesh of a consumer of carrion. His voice now rasped in his throat; its sound clawed at his ears. The hunched, deformed lump of flesh in which he was encased smarted with every movement, as if to constantly remind him that, from this day on, he was conjoined in unholy allegiance with this barren, dusty hellscape. "Is this the experience of humankind?" he asked himself. He resolved to find out.

Pelops rose unsteadily to his feet and, turning his back on the mountain, stumbled and lurched his way down the hillside. The sun rose in the sky, and birds and insects flitted and buzzed in the warming air. Hares darted between thorn bushes, and deer, startled by his sudden appearance, bounded through clearings. Tall trees offered cool shade from the rising sun, and he found himself following an ever-widening path that guided him down the slope of the hill. Soon he heard the splash of water, and the path dipped to ford a stream. Pelops stooped and quenched his thirst. The water was cool; it refreshed him. His heart suddenly lightened, and he stooped to drink more. A thought ran through his mind. 'No nectar ever tasted as good', it rang, causing him to laugh out loud.

He resumed his journey. The trees gave way to a meadow, green and waving in the warm breeze. Flowers of vibrant yellow and soft blue speckled this verdant sea through which the path ploughed a winding course. Pelops was startled by the beauty of the world.

The path continued through the meadow which dipped between lush slopes of pasture. The path swerved towards the stream, and the two, like comfortable traveling companions glided through the long lush valley towards the distant, but glistening sea. Pelops, with increasing confidence, strode out.

The path and stream dipped into a darkened gully, at the far end of which the pasture opened out again. Pelops stopped at the edge of the shade and looked at the sight that greeted his eyes. He saw, a short distance away, where the stream shallowed into a gentle curve, a small collection of stone buildings, a village constructed around a central corral, with animal pens and stacks of hay. Voices, songs, and children's laughter floated toward him on the soft breeze. From his shaded position he could see women at the stream, chatting and laughing as they washed clothes and lay them flat on the warm rocks to dry. Downstream children splashed and gambolled in the shallows, whilst, in the pasture beyond, an assortment of farm animals grazed. In his breast his heart beat with an intensity of joy hitherto unknown, and Pelops smiled in recognition of this newly formed desire to live amongst simple humanity. Pelops stepped into the light.

The screams struck him like shards of flint. A scramble of children, some dragged by their wailing mothers, stampeded towards the village. The approach of Pelops had led to this sudden outburst of fear, and he realised that his sudden appearance from the shadow had startled them. He open his arms to signal his benign intention, but the women screamed even more. He called to them, but the harshness of his voice seemed to distort the meaning of his words. One woman, unencumbered by a child, picked up a stone and threw it at him. Another woman did the same, and then a third. They stood their ground, stooping and hurling, a barrage of stone accompanied by cries of "monster, monster". The stones fell short, but the words struck him.

Then from the meadow beyond the village came the men, charging forward, brandishing the implements of their work. The one who led the charge, a great red-faced ox of a man, wielded a cudgel, and roared. He approached intent on doing Pelops harm, and with both hands, raised the weapon high above his head. Within range, this great bull of a man bought down the club with the intention of crushing the monster's head. Pelops seized the bludgeon in his claw, wrenched it from the man's grasp and tossed it away like a piece of kindling. The man stepped backwards, stumbled, and fell onto his back. His roar turned into a whimper as he squirmed. Pelops looked down at him. The fear in the man's eyes, the quivering terror on his lips, and the skin of his face now blanched the colour of tripe, struck Pelops with a smarting ferocity that no weapon could inflict. He stepped over the sprawling man and strode on. The rest of the men stood at the ready, close to the village entrance, prepared to repel this vile intruder. The women cowered behind them. Pelops turned away from the village and strode onwards along the path. The wailing of the terrified children pursued him as he continued, and a few well aimed stones bounced off his back. When a substantial distance had been gained, and silence surrounded him, Pelops stepped away from the path and sat in a quite bower. Pelops wept.

The day waned, and Pelops moved on. His steps were no longer confident, and his mind blanched at thoughts of human contact. 'Can all people be so fearful of my countenance', he asked himself, 'so cruel in their response to my deformity?' He tried to reason with himself, to talk away the fear of his next human contact. 'Perhaps it was just that one village. Perhaps it was because he stepped unannounced from the shadow. Perhaps the village was suffering from the attacks of brigands, and over-reacted.' In his heart Pelops knew that such suggestions were mere distractions from the truth. He was, he knew, a monster.

Twilight engulfed the land in a blood-red shroud, and the darkness of shadows began to spread across the meadows. Pelops left the path and ascended a steep incline, intent on finding some hidden grove where he could rest for the night. Instead he stepped up onto a dirt road, a well-worn highway rutted by cartwheels. He had not expected to find here such a thoroughfare, and his initial surprise was replaced by mild panic. He did not want to meet anyone unprepared. 'Which way to go?' he asked himself and decided that the approaching night offered more safety than the lingering dusk. A few paces onwards and the glimmer of firelight pierced the bushes to one side of the highway. He smelled the aroma of cooked food, and the aching in his belly began to gnaw. He realised that there were people living here. Yet despite his desperation to call upon them and ask for food he feared another bad encounter. Could he persuade them to give him food, accept his company, treat him as one of their own? Or would they reject him with curses, and chase him away with stones and sticks? He pondered these questions until hunger forced him towards resolution. He decided. 'If I am to be spurned by humankind, then I will be a villain, and take from them that which I want.' With such malevolent intent Pelops went to surge through the thicket towards the light and burst into the clearing beyond, but, at the last moment, a thought overtook him. 'What if I were to employ stealth, and creep silently through the shadows? That way, I would not announce my presence, and they would be caught unawares. Besides,' he continued to muse, 'that way they will not have time to spoil the food before I seize it.' Pelops felt rather proud of himself, for having hatched such a cunning scheme.

Keeping to the darkness, Pelops made his way around the barrier of undergrowth. A path, which revealed itself to him after only a few paces, led from the road towards the firelight. From this dim entrance he could see the fire, and illuminated in the orange glow, an old man sitting at a table. Pelops, crouching low, observed for a few moments the old man. He looked very old, with long grey hair, and an equally long grey beard. He seemed to Pelops, to be very still and quiet. He sat alone in front of what looked, at first glance, to be a hovel, but as his eyes grew accustomed to the firelight, Pelops could see that the little wooden building was more than just a hut. A trellis, covered with vine, enclosed on three sides the table where the old man sat. Large pots stood around, from which sprouted small bushes laden with spring blossom. The fire was set before a stone hearth, and a bubbling, steaming pot, suspended over the flames, emitted enticing aromas.

As Pelops watched, his resolve to steal began to dissolve. The old man sat still and quiet, and Pelops could not imagine that anyone could do harm to such a peaceful creature. After a moment of reflection, Pelops decided to withdraw. 'I would rather go hungry' he thought, 'than do harm to such as he'. With that resolution he turned to creep away, but as he did so, a twig snapped beneath his foot. The old man turned his face toward him and called out. "If you are a friend, draw near. I have food enough to share." Pelops froze. After a silence that seemed to Pelops to hang long in the air, the old man continued. "You have been there some time. I can hear you breathing. If you are a traveller, lost, hungry and tired, you have nothing to fear from me. I am blind and cannot harm you. There is food enough for both of us."

Pelops stood, and stepped into the light. He tried to speak, but his voice croaked in his throat, and he felt embarrassed. He stood with his hands clasped in front of him, his weight shifting from one leg to the other. He looked down at the ground, too embarrassed to look at the blind man.

"Come friend", said the blind man. "The fire is warm, and the food hearty. Come and rest a while. It is dark, and you must be tired."

Pelops sat as he was bidden, and the old man placed before him a goblet of wine. "Drink" he said, and Pelops drank.

The old man served the meal, a stew of game and vegetables. He said that he trapped the game himself and grew his own vegetables. Despite his blindness, he continued to explain, he could move around his garden and the surrounding area. He had lived there all his life, so despite the gradual loss of his sight, he knew with intimate detail the land, where the game grazes in the fields, where the fish swim in the river. His fingers, he continued, knew each of the many fruit trees that he cultivated, and his nose could lead him to the secret places where bees produced their honey. The old man chuckled as he spoke, and Pelops felt a pang of envy for his simple happy life.

They ate the food and drank the wine. Pelops felt a sense of peace. Drowsiness swelled in his breast and he asked the old man where he could sleep. Directed to a room inside the house, he lay on the straw bedding and covered by a warm blanket, fell into a deep sleep.

*

The morning light revealed to Pelops the full beauty, and strange ambience, of the old man's garden. It was undoubtedly tended with care, with each plant fed and watered according to it's need. Yet piled all around, some in dishevelled heaps, some in isolation, were the various parts of several chariots. A wheel here, a horse yoke there, a platform upturned. Some pieces broken, whilst others whole. Some parts appeared to have been strewn thoughtlessly, whilst others appeared to have been placed with careful precision to its immediate environ. The profusion of colour and shape created, for Pelops, a vibrant, yet puzzling arrangement.

The old man appeared from the interior of his home carrying a jug of warm goats' milk. He placed it on the table upon which bread and cheese had already been placed, and invited Pelops to join him for breakfast. The cheese and bread and goats' milk fortified Pelops and when the meal was finished he felt ready for the day. Yet, he was at a loss as to the occupation to pursue. The old man, in anticipation of Pelops' quandary, broached the subject. "What will you do next? he said, and Pelops sat back in contemplation.

"I do not know" he replied. "With my countenance, none will accept me into their company. I am outcast from all of humankind."

"Not all." said the blind man.

"Not all." confirmed Pelops.

"You have not told me your story," the old man said, "and, other than your name, I know nothing about you." Pelops suddenly felt a sense of dread. The subject had not been mentioned the night before, and, for the first time since they met, Pelops realised that the old man, being blind, knew not of his deformity. The talk had focused on the old man's experience, and no reference to Pelops' life had been made. The old man did not know of his ugliness, of his past life feted by the gods, nor of their rejection of him. No question concerning Pelops' journey along this road had been asked, nor answered. For a moment Pelops was at a loss as to what to say.

Pelops quickly decided that the full story might sound incredulous to his host, so he decided on a simpler version. He drew a deep breath and steadied himself. "I was an apprentice charioteer, but was injured, and am now deformed." The simplicity of this statement did nothing to allay his anxiety.

"Where is your home?" asked the old man, and Pelops answered swiftly. "Far beyond Mount Olympus".

"And why did you come this way? Are you intending to challenge Oenomaus?"

Puzzled, Pelops said that he knew nothing of this Oenomaus, and nothing of any challenge. The old man laughed in response, then settled back comfortably in his seat, to set about educating his guest in this subject.

"You have noticed the remnants of many chariots?" he began, "so please allow me to explain to you the reason for their being here. Oenomaus is the king of Pisa, the city to where this road leads. King Oenomaus of Pisa has a beautiful daughter, Hippodamia, and it is said that the intensity of his affection for her borders on the unnatural."

"It has also been prophesised", the old man continued with relish, "that Oenomaus will die by the hand of his son-in-law. Oenomaus, therefore, has devised a scheme to ensure that none could win his daughter's hand. He challenges his daughters' suitors to take Hippodamia in a chariot and ride from Pisa towards Corinth. Sanctuary in that city will guarantee the marriage, but to be overtaken by Oenomaus on the road will mean certain death for the suitor. Eighteen young men have so far accepted the challenge, and eighteen heads are impaled on columns above the King's palace."

"The road from Pisa to Corinth passes here, and these parts, scattered here abouts, are the salvage of those suitors' vehicles. Their horses now run feral; if you were able to construct a chariot from these parts, and could harness a pair of horses, you could challenge the king for his daughter, and, upon his death, you would be king".

Pelops began to contemplate the idea. "If that were possible..."

"It is possible" interrupted the old man with uncharacteristic vehemence. "Oenomaus is a monster. He rules Pisa as a tyrant. He lusts for his own daughter, his own flesh and blood, and he kills any who would love her as he should not. No matter the nature of your injury, no matter the nature of your deformity, you cannot be a greater monster than he who now sits on the throne of Pisa." The old man sat back and rested.

Pelops thought long and hard about what the old man had said. He spent the day ruminating, arguing with himself on the merits of the ordeal, of how it could be achieved, how he, a deformed monster of a near, not quite, man, could compete with the most accomplished charioteer in the region. The pieces that lay about could, he supposed, be put together to build a chariot, but would all these disparate parts work harmoniously? The makers of chariots balanced each component, blended their balance with strength, and matched their strength with flexibility. These parts, lying around and about, the discarded flotsam of failure, could they, he questioned, be forged into a vehicle to rival the best? The sun rose in the sky, hung still through the long noon, then plummeted into dusk. The old man pottered about his garden, attending his vegetables and checking his traps, avoiding contact with his pensive guest, while Pelops sat motionless. As darkness enshrouded the gentle oasis, the old man lit the fire and cooked the evening meal. When it was ready, he served the food. The two companions ate in silence. After draining his wine goblet for the last time that night, the old man said "You can live as you do now, or you can die striving for something greater. Which is worse, to die in the attempt, or sit here and do nothing?" Pelops resolved to compete.

The next day was one of activity. The one-time apprentice of Poseidon had learnt what made a sturdy, dependable, and fast vehicle, and he set to the task with vigour. He balanced yokes with chassis, and platforms with wheels. Just about every component that he could find scattered in the vicinity was enlisted in his endeavour to construct the finest vehicle possible. The chariot that, by the end of the day, he had constructed did not look smart, but it worked smoothly. Pelops knew how to reduce the friction of the wheels against the axles, and how to construct a steering mechanism that reacted with accuracy, an important factor if potholes and wheel-ruts were to be avoided. The next consideration was that of the horses.

During the evening meal the old man told Pelops of the sea cove where, it was said, the chariot horses, now feral, gathered at dawn. He explained that, of course, he had not seen them, his lack of sight disqualifying his certainty of the subject, yet occasional travellers who rested at his home did sometimes mention them. No other chariot horses were available in the district, Oenomaus having reserved them for himself, but, if these feral beasts, having enjoyed freedom from the yoke and who now refused again to be restrained, could be persuaded to serve him, then the sea cove would be the place where they would likely be found. After the meal was finished, Pelops set off in the direction indicated by the old man, resolved to secure for himself, the services of the best.

There was enough moon to guide his way, and just as the eastern sky began to lighten, so Pelops arrived at the sea cove. He secreted himself on a low promontory which offered an uninhibited vista of the entire beach. As the shadows of the night withdrew, the blood red light of dawn illuminated the sea, and the incessantly rolling waves that boomed and foamed onto the land.

As he kept watch, he saw two dark shapes sweep towards the shore and emerge from a crashing wave. Two great seething horses burst through the blood red spume, a primeval nativity of writhing flesh, vigorous, unrestrained, black and glistening in the dawn light. These magnificent looking beasts, snorting and writhing and rearing high as if stretching new-born limbs, bounded across the sand, gambolling with the enthusiasm of the newly unleashed, galloping, kicking, and revelling in their strength.

Pelops stood-up in full view of the finest horses he had ever seen. Upon seeing him standing at the edge of the beach they approached him at the trot, and, stopping before him, bent their massive heads to accept his embrace.

Without the need of a tether or any form of restraint, Pelops led the horses along the road, back to the old man's home. They stopped occasionally to drink from streams, or to graze fresh grass that grew along the way. Farmers in adjoining fields did not run in panic at the sight of the monster and his ferocious entourage, but stood and stared, transfixed by the strange procession. As the sun sank to the horizon, so Pelops and the horses arrived at the old man's home.

As they entered his yard, the old man called out "It sounds and smells like you were successful."

"They are a fine pair, well suited to the task. A gift from Poseidon. I will have to make a sacrifice in recognition of his endowment."

The old man laughed aloud. "A gift from the gods. What a thing to say. Surely you don't believe in that nonsense."

Pelops was taken aback. "The horses came from the sea, a gift from Poseidon for sure. Who else would draw such beasts from the sea, and give them to me to complete my purpose?"

"How can you say such a thing? You are making a joke."

"No" snapped Pelops. "The gods are real. I know."

"What folly you speak, my friend. The voice in your head is your own voice, not the voice of some deity or spirit directing you. It is your own voice, your own thoughts. Don't give me gods. No one has ever seen one, no one has ever spoken to one. They are just stories, myths invented by fools so that the weak can avoid taking responsibility for their own actions. Those horses that you found on the beach are feral and came to you because they need the guidance of a human. There is nothing else to it."

"The gods are real." replied Pelops with rising anger. "I know. I have met them."

The old man scoffed, then said "Let me serve the meal, and then you can tell me all about the gods. Convince me, and I will accept that they do exist, but if you fail, you must admit that you are wrong. Is that fair?"

Pelops swallowed his anger and agreed. The old man served the meal. The horses, without instruction, wandered into an adjacent meadow to graze and rest for the night, and the men settled, to enjoy the food and wine which they both knew would be their last dinner together. As they ate, Pelops, for the first time, told his story.

The old man listened in silence, and when Pelops finished, nodded his head. "My friend" he said, "I will not doubt your word, and I will, therefore, no longer doubt the existence of the gods. Whatever my experience, or lack of such, your story convinces me. Thank you. You have taught this old man a new lesson."

That night, Pelops lay awake beneath the stars, pondering the possibilities that the future could present. Success meant glory, a kingdom, and a wife. Failure meant death. He could not remain as he was, an outcast living on the good grace of an old blind man. He needed to act, for, as the old man had already pointed out, it was better to die than do nothing. The thoughts ran around his mind for hours before, just before dawn, he fell into a shallow sleep.

He awoke, refreshed and calm, to the aroma of warm bread and goats' milk, and the sound of the horses who had returned to the yard. The old man had gathered the breakfast, and the two men sat in silence as they ate. Without a word, Pelops then hitched the horses to the chariot and led them to the entrance. He turned back to look at the old man, who sat at the table, quiet and still, as Pelops had first seen him.

Pelops spoke. "You are the only friend I have in this world. I will miss your company."

The old man thought long. "You are my only friend too." he eventually replied. "I know not what the future holds, neither for you, nor for myself, but I do know that we have both benefited from our friendship. If in the future, you need a quiet place to rest, you will find a home here."

"Thank you" said Pelops, and bowed his head, overcome with an irrational concern, that the blind man would see his tears.

*

The palace of Oenomaus dominated Pisa. Occupying a hill overlooking the tidal estuary where a strategically defendable deep port had been constructed, Pisa was an imposing city of impregnable walls, fortified towers, and an unbreachable gate. The palace, at the high centre of the capital, assured both comfort and safety to whomever occupied its hall. As Pelops rounded the last bend in the road, and the great white stone metropolis revealed itself to his sight, so his desire to win the contest and possess the city blossomed in his breast.

The one road into the city led to an outer keep, a gated bastion guarded by uniformed men-at arms. Merchants and other travellers waited patiently in line to be questioned by an officer as to the nature of their visit to the city. Pelops presumed that such was Oenomaus' fear of assassination that all who came to the city, even the old peasant hags from the farms nearby, had to be vetted before admission to the great citadel. He smirked at the thought of the mighty king quivering at some old crone brandishing a pomegranate. As Pelops approached and the guards focused their attention on him, so some averted their eyes, whilst others visibly winced. The line of visitors waiting at the entrance parted as he approached, and Pelops' smirk twisted into a snarl directed at these weaklings. He drew his chariot into the fortified portal and the officer of the guard approached. "Who are you, and what business have you here?" he demanded in a loud clear voice, as if trying to convince the audience that he was not intimidated by the hideous looking visitor.

Pelops bent forward so that he was speaking into the face of the officer. "Send a messenger to your master Oenomaus, and tell him that I, Pelops, son of king Tantalus, am here to win his daughter's hand."

The expression on the face of the officer eased into a smile, as if he were pleased at the news. He nodded, then instructed a herald to announce the approach of the challenger. A thought struck Pelops, that perhaps Oenomaus was unpopular with his guards and that they would like to see him replaced. An escort was detailed to accompany Pelops to the palace, and they set out at a steady, but unhurried pace. The stone paved streets, enclosed on both sides by terraced houses, wound through the bustling city. Citizens along the way stood silently and stared as the procession passed by. A young girl being carried in her mother's arms began to cry at the sight of the monster, and her mother bent the child's head into her breast, to shield the girl from the hideous sight. An adolescent boy pointed and began to laugh, but a swift and accurate hand clipped the back of his head, and the boy became silent. Pelops, and his escort, arrived at the steps of the palace entrance.

The herald, waiting at the foot of the steps, led Pelops up to the terrace. He announced, in a loud voice, the name of the visitor, and the reason for his visit.

The scene on the terrace appeared to Pelops as contrived, as if the king had prepared for such meetings as this, and his entire entourage rehearsed in the parts that they were to play. Oenomaus, lounging on golden cushions set on a vast white marble seat that faced towards the grand vista of the city, continued an intimate conversation with a high-ranking minion, whilst courtiers, clustered in small groups, drinking from golden goblets, selecting slivers of exquisitely prepared food from gold platters offered to them by attendants, conversed in soft tones. On the far side of the great marble chair, a group of female attendants, including at least one matron and two nurses, stood in silence. The centre of this group was occupied by a young woman who stood with her back towards the centre so that her face was concealed from the visitor. The threads of spun gold woven through her hair, however, identified her as the princess, Hippodamia. All appeared unconcerned by the arrival of a new challenger.

A long moment passed before the king turned to face the newcomer. His colour immediately drained to ashen white as he froze into the expression of horror. The minion beside him gasped, and a female courtier let out a quickly stifled cry. Hippodamia turned. She too turned white at the sight of the monster and fell to the floor in a dead faint. Chaos ensued. A scurry of nurses and attendants tried to revive the fallen princess. An attendant stepped backwards in horror and released his grip on the large gold platter, laden with succulent morsels, which he, at that moment, had been offering to guests. It clattered onto the marble floor and sent a fountain spray of crimson source cascading over a large group of Pisa's nobility. One of their number, her face awash with red, leaned over the balcony, and retched. Courtiers and attendants stampeded in a pandemonium of movement. Oenomaus alone remained as still as a stone effigy, paralysed with fear.

Pelops stepped forward and spoke. "Mighty king Oenomaus, the magnificence of your court is legendary. I thank you for your welcome. I feel as if I have found my true home."

Oenomaus sat and stared.

Pelops continued "Your daughter, the princess Hippodamia is more beautiful than the legends tell."

The look of fright on the face of the king changed to that of panic. "My... my daughter..." he stammered.

"Your daughter, mighty king," continued Pelops, "Fair, beautiful. It is little wonder that so many suitors have sought her hand in marriage. I, too, am here to win her. If the fates are willing, I will soon call her wife, and you, father".

“You.... You...” replied Oenomaus. His eyes darted around the terrace, seeking support from some quarter. None came.

“Yes, me.” Pelops turned and addressed the now transfixed audience. “I am Pelops, son of Tantalus, king of Sipylus. I will prove myself a worthy suitor for the princess Hippodamia and am prepared for any challenge that the mighty king Oenomaus can demand of me.”

Oenomaus steadied himself against the great marble seat and stood. “You...,” he shouted, pointing in the direction of Pelops, “You cannot marry my daughter. You..., you..., look at you... You are a..., not a..., not a man.”

The assembly gasped.

“Not a man,” repeated Pelops. “Not a man you say. Mighty king. Perhaps the excitement of the occasion has affected your vision, or your consciousness, or your reason. Do you not see me standing before you, the son of Tantalus, the prince of Sipylus? I am a man, full in strength and vigour, and wit. I will marry your daughter, mighty king, and you will call me son.”

“Never” shouted the king. “You are not a man. You are an abomination. Why the gods allow such as you to continue roaming this earth is a mystery to me. But I do know this. You are not fit to marry my daughter, nor to rule this kingdom after me.”

Both men glared at the other as if they would join in deathly combat. The tension of the moment entombed the onlookers in a numbing paralysis. The intensity of the tension seemed to increase, and just as if the two men were about to launch an attack upon the other, so a courtier, the one with whom Oenomaus was in conversation at the arrival of Pelops, stepped forward, and addressed the king.

"My king," said he, adopting a light tone, "he who stands before you is, as he proclaims himself to be, a prince, a worthy suitor for your daughter, Hippodamia. But you, mighty king, are the foremost charioteer in the land. There can be no doubt that this... this... worthy prince is sincere in his desire to accept the challenge of the race. There can be no doubt as to the outcome of the challenge. One more head to grace the roof of your palace, mighty king, would not be, how shall I say it?... excessive?"

Oenomaus relaxed back into the great marble seat and laughed. The tension of the moment shattered like ice, and colour began to return to the face of the king.

"Yes of course," he replied, and waved his hand as if flicking away a bothersome gnat. "Yes, my wise counsellor. The challenge. Yes, this... this... near man cannot complete the challenge." He turned his attention to Pelops. "You know of the challenge, the race to Corinth?"

Pelops said that he did.

"Then tomorrow you can prove yourself worthy of my daughter, and my kingdom... eh... Pelops?... yes.... Tomorrow, we will conclude this matter. Until then, you may find food for your horses, and warm straw for your bed in the stables. I will have a boy show you to them. I quite understand if you should have a change of heart during the night and leave the city. I will ensure that an escort is available to convey you safely through the dark streets, should you wish to leave. But, if you draw your chariot to the city gates just as the morning sun tops the far mountains, then you will learn to understand what it takes to be a real man."

Pelops said nothing. He bowed to the king, turned, and followed an attendant down the steps, the pounding of his heart restricting his breath.

The stable boy into whose care Pelops had been placed, was keen to prove to his guest the vast reaches of his knowledge of the name, age, and parentage, of every horse in the vast stable.

Pelops led his fine pair past all the king's horses and settled them in the stall indicated by the boy. Fresh water, quality feed, and warm bedding awaited the animals. The boy had, alongside almost the entire domestic staff of the royal household, watched the arrival of the new challenger. They were, continued the boy with an exuberance that, rare in one so young, delighted his audience, that the palace staff were shouting for the challenger.

Pelops was given an end stall next to his horses. The hay was warm and plentiful, and there was a pair of rough blankets, freshly laundered. It soon became apparent that this was the stall where the boy slept.

"To keep out the dawn chill," explained the boy, casting a blanket towards his guest.

"You know much about these horses. I am impressed" said Pelops as they settled into the straw. "I expect that you can't wait until you are training them yourself".

"Oh no," replied the boy, the smile on his face falling away. "The king doesn't allow anyone to drive them. Nobody but Myrtilus."

"Who is this Myrtilus?" asked Pelops, and the boy told all he knew.

"Myrtilus is the king's charioteer. He drives one pair each day, in rotation. This way, one team is fresh each morning. Tomorrow is the turn of the dappled pair, taken from Lycurgus. Today, it was the white stallions of Aristomachus, so they are the pair at their peak. I expect Myrtilus will prepare the chariot for the morning. Only he may touch the vehicles, unless it's me, after training, to clean them."

"Is he good to you, this Myrtilus?"

"No. He's a mean, bad, mean..."

"You said mean twice."

"Well he is. He thinks he's better than everyone else who works here, but he is not better than anyone. He's an attendant, just like everyone else. And he's got a secret."

"A secret?" Pelops sat up. "Do tell me his secret."

The boy looked at Pelops and laughed. "I cannot tell you his secret. It wouldn't be a secret if I told you."

Pelops thought for a moment, considered his options, and opted for the following tactic.
"How did this secret come to you?" he asked.

"I heard the cook and the housekeeper talking about it. The housekeeper said that she had listened to Myrtilus doing something to himself that I didn't understand, and he kept saying the name of Oenomaus' daughter,

Hippodamia. Cook told me it was a secret and that I shouldn't tell anybody."

"That is useful information." said Pelops and settled back into a reverie.

"Are you hungry?" The boys chatter interrupted his thoughts. "Cook said that she hasn't been told to provide for you. I told her you could share mine. The smell from the kitchen says that something is ready. Stay here and I will bring you something. If Myrtilus comes, keep a low profile. He is a mean... bad... mean..." The boy disappeared into the gloom, leaving Pelops in the warmth of the horses.

With what seemed to Pelops a very short time, the boy returned with two large bowls of fish stew, a loaf of warm bread, and the promise of more if Pelops were still hungry. The whole of the domestic staff, minus Myrtilus, had donated to his meal.

Pelops asked if the king dined on the same dish, but the boy said that he did not. "He has his own kitchen, with a cook who lives inside the castle. They say he is a prisoner, a hostage against poisoning. Oenomaus, cook says, fears his own shadow."

"Yet he has eighteen heads on spikes above his roof."

"Cook says they are the heads of boys."

Drowsiness overtook the boy, and folding himself into the straw, fell into a deep sleep. Pelops stretched out and closed his eyes. Strange images wove dreams he did not understand, then a voice, soft and furtive, bought him back from the deep. From shadows the soft voice carried to the ears of

Pelops... "...impossible... ...countenance the possibility... ...born deformed. Should my father falter, and I am at the mercy of the beast, I would rather you, than he, spawn my..."

A stern voice broke in. "I cannot do as you bid. I cannot stand by and watch you with that... that..."

"What can you do? You are not a prince or a nobleman. You cannot kill the king and replace him. You would be flayed alive in the public square by those who would then fall upon each other's throats to take me. If he wins, then I am his. Everything is his. Give me one chance, one hope, one night, to satisfy me for the rest of my life."

"One night? I could not live with just one night. I would rather starve myself of joy, than curse myself to one memory. Without a kingdom, I cannot have you. Find another, many would be willing."

Footsteps, guided by lamplight, faded through the stable. A soft groan came into Pelops' consciousness, quickly followed by long moaning. A howl ensued, and a man wept in the darkness, as if his heart was breaking. Eventually the crying abated, easing to soft moaning, then silence.

Pelops made his move. Emerging from the darkness, he stepped into the stall in which the king's charioteer lay cowering in a corner. As Pelops entered, so Myrtilus strove to stand. He grasped the rail and hauled himself to his feet whilst trying to hide his tears. He stood before Pelops, shaking, and ashen. "What do you want?" he demanded.

"What do you want?" answered Pelops. "I know what I want, but I don't know what you want, or do I? I heard what you said to the fair maiden. Is she what you want?"

Myrtilus seethed. "I serve the king. I would do nothing disloyal, nor dishonourable, nor disturbing of the king's rule."

"But what if you were the king, or a king, shall we say?"

"A king?"

"Yes, a king. Suppose I win the race and marry Hippodamia. I could give half of the kingdom to whomever assured my victory. Half my kingdom. You could be king Myrtilus."

"How could I trust you to fulfil your side of the bargain?"

"It's your decision, if you trust me, or not. If you do trust me, there is an additional service you could render, which you couldn't do if you were anything less than a king."

"Tell me."

"Hippodamia is concerned that my children will be deformed like me. I too, have such concern. To alleviate this concern, I believe that it would be in our interests to do all that we can to ensure that my heir inherits nothing from me but my kingdom. To that end, I will select a fit and able man to sire a child by her. He will take her virginity, and do that which is necessary, and for as long as necessary, to give her a child. That man would have to be a king. That man could be you."

Myrtilus withdrew back into the corner, his skin red hot, his eyes alive with fiendish brilliance.

He tried to speak, but words would not form in his gaping mouth. Pelops turned away.

The new dawn witnessed great activity. By the time Pelops drew his chariot to the gates, a crowd had gathered, and onlookers were lining the route. The herald announced the arrival of the challenger, and as Pelops stepped down from his vehicle, so Oenomaus appeared on the first-floor balcony. He gave a soft signal, a gentle flick of the hand, and a standard was raised. All heads turned towards the direction of the stable. All was still, only the trill squabbling of sparrows pierced the silence of the collective tension. Then suddenly, a thunder of charging hooves announced the coming of the king's chariot. Myrtilus rounded into view, two great white stallions drawing a mighty chariot. With the ability of the true master of horse, Myrtilus swiftly halted before the king, and dismounted.

Oenomaus descended the steps, accompanied by his loyal entourage.

"My horses look splendid this morning, Myrtilus." pronounced Oenomaus. "You do me great service. Of all my servants, I consider you above the rest."

The king stepped forward, but Myrtilus stood in his way. "My king," he said, "there is one task left for me to do, in order to complete the preparations of the chariot. The axle pins need to be replaced. I have freshly forged pins to replace those that are in place but are worn. I intend to give the finest service to my king." Pelops observed that, for a moment, Oenomaus appeared uneasy. Yet he nodded his consent.

As he completed the maintenance, Myrtilus saw in his mind an image of the beautiful Hippodamia coming to him in the chamber of his palace. With deft movements, he removed the bronze pins and replaced them with counterfeits made from bee's wax. When finished, he bowed to the king.

Oenomaus wound the reins of his steeds tightly around his wrists. He mounted the vehicle and stood poised to begin. He signalled to Hippodamia to join her suitor for the dash to Corinth, as was the established custom, but the princess remained at the top of the steps. Oenomaus accepted her choice, and called to Pelops to depart for Corinth, and safety.

When Pelops whipped-up his horses, he carefully aimed his whip-strike above their flanks and reined in their enthusiasm for speed to a deceptively steady pace. For the spectators at the starting line, the roar of Pelops as the vehicle lurched forward, and the dust kicked up by the hooves and wheels, confirmed their belief that he strove for distance. He rounded the first bend, slowed, then halted. He waited in the lee of a copse.

He did not need to wait long, for soon the thunder of horse's hooves came to him from the direction of the city. Yet above that thunderous beat, another sound, a scream, high pitched and desperate in its constancy, accompanied the equine timpani.

Around the bend galloped the horses of Oenomaus, harnessed in the chariots yoke, yet minus the body of the vehicle. In its stead, Oenomaus, still bound to the horse's reins, was being dragged. His knees and elbows were already flayed, yet his consciousness remained. As the awful spectacle rounded the bend, so the body of Oenomaus twisted and rolled onto its back. Pelops waited for them to pass, then bid his horses forward.

Oenomaus, now looking up and back, saw the horses of Pelops bearing down on him. He found the strength to reel away from their pounding hooves, but exhaustion and debilitating pain slowed his reactions. Pelops heard the screams and felt the cool wind-whipped blood-burst mist strike his chest and face. Within a few seconds the torso of the once proud king burst open, and the shoulders separated from the arms. The head of the king rolled into the ditch.

Oenomaus' horses slowed to a trot, then stopped. Pelops halted and released them from their horrific tether. As a man who knew the value of a matched pair of chariot horses, Pelops was delighted with the first possession of his rule. He turned back towards the city and halted, again, to retrieve the head of his adversary.

Pelops returned to the city to ascend the throne and possess his wife. Hippodamia had remained at the bastion, at the top of the balcony steps in the hope of watching her father return. Instead, Pelops, drenched in blood, entered the keep. He hurled the head of Oenomaus at the foot of the steps, descended the chariot, and, stepping over the gruesome memento, climbed towards his future. Hippodamia fainted.

When she recovered from her faint, Hippodamia began to twitch and writhe, and moan and wail. Her matron suggested that sedatives be administered, and that she would soon recover her countenance. With Hippodamia as his wife, no legitimate challenge against his right to the throne could be made. The ceremony, Pelops decided, needed to be completed before the drugs stopped working.

*

Pelops moved quickly to organise the ceremony of celebration for his ascension to the throne of Pisa. He removed the leering skulls of Hippodamia's previous suitors from their places on the walls and exhumed their hastily buried bodies. He organised for them an honourable ceremony of remembrance and erected a monument in their collective memory. He next commissioned the construction of a new hippodrome where regular chariot races in honour of the gods of Olympus would be inaugurated. Then he turned his attention to Hippodamia, and to their wedding night.

The event was meticulously organised. The king's cook had already been released from his confinement, and Pelops had directed that all the food eaten in the palace be prepared in the same kitchen. This proved popular with the staff, who set to the task of preparation with enthusiasm. Invitations were dispatched to neighbouring kings. The day before the wedding was a day of bustling activity, with the arrival of guests and their entourages, and deliveries of food and wine being particularly irksome. But the staff worked well together, and Pelops was pleased. “Only one more task” he said to himself as night settled in, closing the arduous day. He crept to the stable, were he found Myrtilus seated on a grand wooden chair, draped with the worn-out cushions discarded from the palace. He looked every inch the king of the stable. He had been drinking, heavily, guessed Pelops, as the aroma of spilt wine and urine stung his nostrils. Wine stains had bled into Myrtilus’ shirt, a result of Myrtilus having missed his mouth. The sudden appearance of Pelops startled him.

“You celebrate your last night as a servant alone?” asked Pelops as he stepped into the light. He could see, through the staring eyes, that the gall was already rising in Myrtilus’ spleen. He continued, delighting in the opportunity to exploit the limited intellectual capacity of the dead king’s favourite. “I am here to remind you of the responsibility that you swore to undertake. You have proved yourself to be worthy of your future, and I intend that that future begins tomorrow night. Are you up to the challenge, Myrtilus? Can you fulfil the duty of a king?”

Myrtilus smirked a drunken smirk, then nodded his head.

Pelops continued. "I shall send her to you, in the watch tower. During the feasting, she will take her leave, escorted by her entourage to my chamber. From there she shall be escorted to you. The two of you will be left alone together. I shall see to it that cushions, and soft blankets be arrayed according to... to... need I say it?"

Myrtilus belched.

"I don't expect you to be so relaxed tomorrow. A drunk is no good to me. You be sober, and you be awake. Don't disappoint."

Myrtilus looked straight at Pelops. "I can do what I can do, and I can do it best" he said, before slipping back into his wine induced torpor.

Pelops returned, unmissed, to his hall.

The ceremony, the next day, progressed smoothly, due in no small part to the skills of the nurses and matrons who sedated Hippodamia with soothing unctions. At the appointed time, late in the evening that was devoted to feasting and celebration, Hippodamia was led away from the hall by her attendants and placed comfortably in Pelops' bedchamber. The new husband thanked his guests for joining him in this happy occasion and toasted their health. They, in their turn, encouraged him with coarse songs and ribald jokes, to fulfil his husbandly duty. The entire company were blessed with joyous memories of Pelops departing the hall. Many of them remained feasting and drinking until they passed out. None were aware of the true intention of Pelops.

The watch tower stood alone, it's back to the sea, high upon the cliff wall. Intended as a last desperate redoubt, the aura of the building was bleak. That night, however, the warm light of a lamp shone from the highest chamber of the tower, though none of the revellers noticed. Prepared in the expediency of the arrival of an unexpected guest, Myrtilus followed the instructions of Pelops, and was now installed on the cushions. The wine that was awaiting him was plentiful, of the finest quality, and he had drunk with vigour. When first he had arrived, he was pleased with the way the chamber had been prepared. Now, as the night dragged on and the anticipation of the ecstasy to come wore off, the intoxicated boredom of waiting began to make him nervous. He lay still on his back, closed his eyes, and dreamt of Hippodamia.

It was the softest of creaks, the gentlest grating of hinge and wood. The door opened and closed, a sylph of moonlight shadow slipped across the wall and floor, and Myrtilus was aware that the object of his desire, the focus of his love, the fair Hippodamia, awaited him on the balcony. He rose to his feet, and stepped, lurching slightly with the effects of fine wine, towards the moonlight bathed balcony.

Pelops stepped into the light.

Myrtilus froze. Even in the cold moonlight, Pelops could read the expressions on Myrtilus' face as they passed from surprise, through the realisation of his foolishness, and the anger such realisation causes, through resistance, through resignation, and finally, to despair. Myrtilus knew then that he was a fool. He began to grizzle.

"I must thank you for the part you played in my ascension." said Pelops. "I could not have done it without you."

Myrtilus stared at Pelops. A torrent of hate flashed wildly from his eyes. Myrtilus knew that he was beaten. "I don't understand why you had to deceive me. I would have served you. I would have been as good to you as I was to Oenomaus." he snivelled.

"You killed Oenomaus. What good are you to me?"

"I killed him for you."

"You killed him for Hippodamia. You killed him for love."

"Yes, for love. I love Hippodamia. I have loved her always. She should be mine. She should be... be..."

"But she's not yours," said Pelops, "she's mine."

Myrtilus stood at the rail and looked out over the sea. He stared straight ahead towards the distant horizon, to where the dark sky touched the moon reflecting water. Quivering shudders rippled through his shoulders as he wept. "What will you do with me now?" he said with the voice of the bullied, tormented boy that he once was. "I could go away, where no one could find me."

"Yes," said Pelops, "that is exactly where you are going."

Myrtilus turned to face Pelops, and in that moment, realised what that last remark really meant. He raised his fist and lurched forward to strike Pelops and, by so doing, undo all the failures of his life. His blow lacked vehemence, and it failed to strike the target. Myrtilus instead found himself in the grasp of the monster, first dragged, then lifted, finally pushed. Myrtilus, too drunk to resist, was now balanced over the edge of the rail, clinging to the embrace of Pelops for his life. With a last effort, he arched his back and, bending his mouth to Pelops' ear, whispered the curse. Then he relaxed.

His body, now minus tension, slipped from his captor's grip. At peace with himself, Myrtilus tumbled and span through the air. He crashed onto the rocks below, not realising, that he had slurred his words.

Pelops returned to the feasting.

www.ingramcontent.com/pod-product-compliance
Ingram Content Group UK Ltd.
Pitfield, Milton Keynes, MK11 3LW, UK
UKHW020229250726
13967UKWH00001B/271

9 781916 382206